PET SHOW!

For Susan Hirschman

PUFFIN BOOKS
Published by the Penguin Group
Penguin Putnam Books for Young Readers, 345 Hudson Street, New York, New York 10014, U.S.A.
Penguin Books Ltd, 27 Wrights Lane, London W8 5TZ, England
Penguin Books Australia Ltd, Ringwood, Victoria, Australia
Penguin Books Canada Ltd, 10 Alcorn Avenue, Toronto, Ontario, Canada M4V 3B2
Penguin Books (N.Z.) Ltd, 182-190 Wairau Road, Auckland 10, New Zealand

Penguin Books Ltd, Registered Offices: Harmondsworth, Middlesex, England

First published in the United States of America by the Macmillan Company, 1972
First Aladdin Paperbacks edition, 1987
Published by Viking and Puffin Books, divisions of Penguin Putnam Books for Young Readers, 2001

27 28 29 30

Copyright © Ezra Jack Keats, 1972

LIBRARY OF CONGRESS CATALOGING-IN-PUBLICATION DATA
Keats, Ezra Jack.
Pet show / by Ezra Jack Keats.
p.   cm.
Summary: When he can't find his cat to enter in the neighborhood pet
show, Archie must do some fast thinking to win a prize.
ISBN 978-0-670-03504-5 (hardcover)—ISBN 978-0-14-230000-8 (pbk.)
[1. Pet shows—Fiction. 2. Pets—Fiction.] I. Title.
PZ7.K2253 Pc 2001   [E]—dc21 00-012377

Manufactured in China

EZRA JACK KEATS

PET SHOW!

PUFFIN BOOKS

Everyone was talking about the pet show.

The kids told each other
about the pets they would bring.
Matt said he would bring ants!
"I'm gonna bring my mouse!" bragged Roberto.
"What are you gonna bring, Archie—the cat?"
"Uh-huh," said Archie.

The next day they all got ready for the pet show.
"Where's the cat?" Archie called.
"Anyone see the cat?"
Archie and Willie looked in the cat's
favorite hangouts, while Peter and Susie
searched up and down the street.
No cat.

Archie's mother came to the window.
"Where can that cat be?" he asked her.
"You know how independent he is, Archie.
You never know when to expect him."
"But I expect him now! It's time for the pet show!
Maybe he's inside somewhere."
Archie ran into the building.

After a while he came to the window.
"I can't find him. I looked all over the place.
You'd better start without me."
"Gee, we're sorry, Archie," said Peter.
"So long," said Susie.

They got to the entrance.
A lot of people were already there.
Just then, Roberto's mouse took off.

Willie chased the mouse.
Roberto chased Willie.
Peter chased Roberto.
Susie chased Peter—
and the show started.

"Line up with your pets, please!"
the judges called.
They walked up and down, looking carefully
at every pet, and asking, "How old is your pet?"
and "What's your pet's name?"

Everyone got a prize for something.
There was the noisiest parrot,
the handsomest frog, the friendliest fishes,
the yellowest canary, the busiest ants,

the brightest goldfish, the longest dog,
the fastest mouse, the softest puppy,
the slowest turtle—
and many more!

As the last prize was being awarded,
someone shouted,
"Look—here comes Archie!"

"Hello. You're just in time!" a judge said.
"What's in that bag?"
"My pet."
"May I see it, please?"
At that moment the cat showed up.

The other judge called out, "A blue ribbon to the nice lady for the cat with the longest whiskers!"

Before anyone could say anything, he pinned
a blue ribbon on the old woman and came back to Archie.

"What kind of a pet have you got in that jar?"

"A germ!" answered Archie.

"Mmmm—and what's your germ's name?"

Archie thought for a moment.

"Al," he said.

The judges whispered to each other.

"A blue ribbon for Al, the quietest pet in the show!" the judges announced.

As everyone was leaving,
the old woman came over to Archie.
"He's really your cat, isn't he?" she said.
"You should have the ribbon."
"It's OK," Archie said. "You keep it."
And he ran to join his friends.

They passed the old woman on their way home.

"Thank you for the ribbon," she called.

Archie smiled.

"It looks good on you. See you around."

"See you around," she said.